and the New Baby

BBC CHILDREN'S BOOKS

One morning, Pingu was sitting reading his favourite comic when he heard Mum and Dad talking in excited voices on the other side of the room. It's that egg again, thought Pingu to himself. Mum and Dad always seemed to be fussing over it. Pingu carried on reading.

Mum and Dad had been sitting on the egg to keep it warm for a long time, but today something was different.

"I'm sure I felt it move," Dad told Mum. "Do you think it's about to hatch?"

"Oh, my goodness," said Mum, anxiously. "Get off it quickly and let's have a look."

Dad got up off the egg and looked at it. Sure enough, it was beginning to bulge and roll around as if something inside was determined to get out.

Pingu looked up from his comic again. This time he couldn't believe his eyes. He stared at the bulging egg and knew that at last his new baby brother or sister would soon be here.

Then, at the same moment, the kettle began to whistle and the phone started to ring. Suddenly everything seemed to be happening at once.

Pingu went to answer the phone, but Dad stopped him. "Leave it, Pingu," fussed Dad. "We're far too busy to talk to anyone."

"But I can't stand all this noise," said Pingu and he started to cry.

Mum stepped in. She took the kettle off the heat and picked up the phone. "We're very busy today," she said. "Please ring back tomorrow."

Then she went to comfort Pingu. "Everything's all right," she told him. "And just think, in a short while, you'll have a little baby to play with."

Suddenly there was a loud yelp from Dad who was sitting on the egg again.

"Ouch!" he shouted and leapt up in the air. Something orange had poked its way through the shell and prodded Dad right in the bottom!

"Go and ring the midwife and tell her to come quickly. We'll need her help to get the baby out of the egg," Mum shouted to Dad in an extremely worried voice.

Dad rang the midwife who said she would come straight away.

While Mum got things ready, Pingu decided to go and wait for the midwife outside. He stood on the roof and shouted across the snow.

"Midwife, hurry up! Our new baby is about to arrive!"

In no time at all the midwife came rushing along
on her skates. Pingu opened the door for her and she
went zooming in . . .

. . . only to collide with Dad who was waiting for her near the door.

"I'm so sorry," she said. "It's these skates. I always have trouble stopping."

The midwife got straight to work. She fished her stethoscope out of her bag and listened to the sounds the baby was making inside the egg.

"Oh, yes," she said. "This one is ready to come out all right."

Mum and Dad looked on anxiously.

Meanwhile, Pingu had got hold of the midwife's hat. He put it on and shouted at everyone.

"Look at me! It's Pingu the midwife."

But nobody seemed at all interested. They were gazing intently at the egg.

So Pingu went right up to the table where everyone was bending over the egg and tried again.

"Hallo," he said cheerfully. "It's Pingu the midwife here. Can I help?"

Dad looked at him crossly, took off the hat and pushed him away from the table.

"This is no time for fooling around, Pingu," he snapped. "We're all *very* busy. Now keep away and just play quietly outside on your own."

"I don't want to," Pingu shouted. "Why can't I watch, too? It's not fair."

"Shh!" whispered Dad.

The midwife had now got out
her spoon and was tapping
the egg very gently. The shell
was starting to crack.

Two orange feet
appeared and Mum
and Dad cooed
excitedly.

Pingu couldn't bear all this fuss. No one seemed interested in him any more. They only cared about that stupid egg and every time *he* tried to have a look at it they pushed him away or told him to be quiet. It was all too much for Pingu and he started to cry. But still no one took any notice.

Pingu tried once again to see what was going on, but this time Mum and Dad spread out their flippers so he couldn't catch so much as a glimpse of what was happening. Instead all he could do was pace impatiently up and down behind them. This baby was certainly taking a long time to arrive.

And then suddenly, Mum and Dad smiled happily at one another and stood back proudly to let Pingu see the new baby.

"I've got a sister!" exclaimed Pingu. "Hallo!
I'm your brother."

The new baby gurgled with pleasure and
began to suck one of her feet.

"I think the baby has a dirty bottom," Pingu told the midwife importantly.

"You're right," said the midwife, having a look. "Perhaps you can help me clean her up."

The midwife wiped the baby's bottom clean and then gave the dirty cloth to Pingu.

"Would you throw this away for me?" she said.

Pingu took the cloth and put it in the toilet. Then he pulled the chain. Looking after a baby is hard work, he thought to himself.

It was time for the midwife to go.

"Thank you for everything," said Mum and Dad.

"Any time," said the midwife and she skated out of the door.

Mum and Dad bent over to admire the new baby.

"You'll have to stop smoking that smelly old pipe now that we have a baby in the house," said Mum.

"I know who might like the pipe," said Pingu and he took it outside for the snowman.

27

Dad rocked the baby in his arms.
"I think we'll call you Pinga," he said, gazing adoringly at his new baby daughter.

Mum gave Pinga a nice warm bottle of milk.
"She must be hungry after all that hard work
hatching out of her shell," she said.

Dad started to set up his camera.

"What we need is a nice family picture now that our new baby is here," he said.

Everyone lined up in front of the camera. Pingu put on his best camera smile and tried to look as handsome as possible.

Flash, went the camera!
And here is the photo that
Dad's camera took.
Don't they look a
happy family?

More delightful Pingu stories to read
and favourite characters to collect

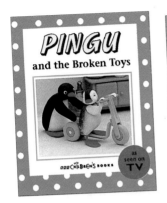

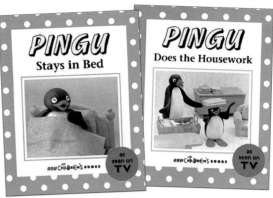

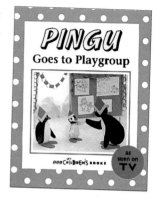

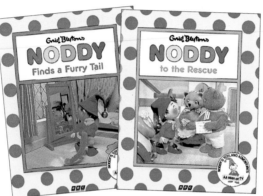

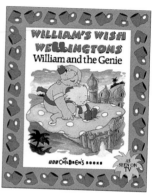

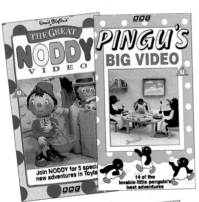

BBC CHiLDReN'S PUBLISHING